Where
Is Coco
Going?

WHERE IS COCO GOING?

by Sloane Tanen

photographs by Stefan Hagen

BLOOMSBURY
CHILDREN'S
BOOKS

Published by Bloomsbury, New York and London
Distributed to the trade by Holtzbrinck Publishers
Library of Congress Cataloging-in-Publication Data available upon request
ISBN 1-58234-951-7

First U.S. Edition 2004
Printed in Hong Kong/China
1 3 5 7 9 10 8 6 4 2

Bloomsbury USA Children's Books
175 Fifth Avenue
New York, NY 10010

All papers used by Bloomsbury Publishing are natural, recyclable products
made from wood grown in well-managed forests. The manufacturing processes conform
to the environmental regulations of the country of origin.

dedicated to **NORMAN** and **CELIA KIRMAN**

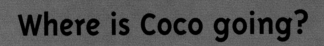

Where is Coco going?

In a taxi that's stuck in traffic . . .

On a train that's way too slow . . .

On a skateboard that's going faster . . .

Where is Coco going?

Through the desert on a hot, hot day . . .

Passing through a scary forest . . . .

"YIPES!" Where is Coco going?

Up in the sky enjoying the weather . . .

In a spaceship and getting close . . .

Trains, planes, spaceships, AND a parachute???

Where **IS** Coco going?

GRANDMA'S HOUSE!!!

Acknowledgments

Grateful acknowledgment to Tracy James and Coco Nelson for all of their inspiration.
I'd also like to thank Stefan Hagen, who, once again, outdid himself with these incredible photographs.
My gratitude to Matthew Lenning for the great design, to Trudell for lending us her talents in creating the scary forest,
to Gary Oshust for his model-making skills, and to The Tiny Doll House and The Doll House Lady for always being well-stocked.
Finally, thanks to my family, and to Amy Williams, Colin Dickerman, Victoria Wells Arms, and the entire staff at Bloomsbury.
...Oh, and to Beth Altschull, for I don't know what, but she wasn't happy
about not being thanked in the last book.